the T·i·n · H·e·a·r·t

the Tin Heart

by Karen Ackerman / illustrated by Michael Hays

Atheneum 1990 New York

Mahaley Hutchison and her family lived along the bank of the
Ohio River in a spot people called "the Point." It was a good place
to cross the river because the water there was calm and smooth.
Her father ran a ferryboat from the Ohio side of the river to the
Kentucky side and back again. The ferryboat was named the
Belle of the Point, and Mahaley's father had painted the name in
red letters across the wooden sides of the boat.

The *Belle* was a long, wide boat with a small steam engine at

the stern. On the deck, Mahaley's father had built a long, fenced corral and several large crates for the animals people took across the river.

Mahaley helped her father by collecting the fares from passengers who brought horses and buggies or wagons on board for the river crossing. The fare was one penny for each person, two cents for each wagon or buggy, and a nickel for a small herd of cows, goats, or sheep. She carried a metal coin box on a leather shoulder strap to keep the money in.

The family living on the Kentucky side of the river across from the Point was named Scotchman, and their daughter Flora was Mahaley's best friend. The *Belle of the Point* came ashore at a pier called "Scotchman's Dock," and Flora's father ran a supply store there for travelers needing food or dry goods for their journey.

Mahaley and Flora had been best friends for as long as either one could remember. Each day, people crossed the river on the *Belle* to do business on one side or the other, or to visit someone on one side or the other, and while passengers unloaded their belongings or animals at Scotchman's Dock, Mahaley and Flora played together. Sometimes the two girls swam in a shallow stream that ran behind the Scotchman home.

Flora's father had once been a tinsmith's apprentice, and he made something special for Flora and Mahaley to share. He hammered a little heart out of tin, cut it exactly in two, and he gave each of them one half to wear on a piece of twine around her neck.

He told them it was a friendship heart, and no matter where they were, the tin heart meant they were friends. Flora and Mahaley each wore the half of their tin friendship heart from that day on and never took it off, not even in the washtub.

By the summer of 1860, whole families began to cross the river on the *Belle*, with all they owned packed in one wagon. Many of them crossed the river because of the rumors that the Northern states and Southern states would fight a war over slavery, and they wanted to be close to their relatives before the war began.

The *Belle of the Point* became more crowded each day with people who wanted to go to the South or to the North. The Hutchisons and Scotchmans worked very hard, one family taking passengers across the river and the other selling them whatever they might need on the road. Soon there were so many passengers, the *Belle* was full on every trip, and Scotchman's store ran out of salt and sugar and beef jerky.

When the Civil War started, people on both sides of the river argued about slavery. There were some who tried to help runaway slaves cross the river to the North, and some who tried to stop them from crossing.

Although Kentucky had voted against slavery, many people there still believed that slavery was right. Often, fathers, sons, and brothers stood around Mr. Scotchman's store in the afternoons, arguing about the war. Sometimes tempers got too hot, and Flora's father would have to go outside to stop a fistfight.

Mahaley and Flora didn't worry about the war at first, and they played together just the same whenever the *Belle* pulled into Scotchman's dock. But something was wrong between their fathers.

Mr. Hutchison hung the Northern flag from the cabin roof of the *Belle*, and Mr. Scotchman hung the Southern flag on a pole in front of his supply store. The two men hardly spoke to each other, because each of them felt differently about the war.

One day, a group of men standing near the supply store at Scotchman's Dock wouldn't let the *Belle of the Point* tie up at the pier to pick up passengers bound for the Northern states.

"Take your boat home, Yankee!" they yelled at Mahaley's father, and they threw stones from the shore at the boat.

"We won't be docking here again," Mahaley's father told her as he turned the *Belle* back to the Ohio side of the river, leaving the people standing on Scotchman's Dock. As the *Belle* chugged away, Mahaley and Flora waved to each other. Each girl held her half of the tin friendship heart tightly, knowing it might be a long time before they could play together again.

One evening, as Mahaley helped her
mother bake biscuits for supper,
someone knocked on the Hutchisons'
door. Mahaley peeked out from behind
the homespun curtain that separated
the kitchen from the other three small
rooms of the house. A tall man in shiny
black boots and a black hat spoke to her
father quietly at the doorway.

"Will you help us?" the man asked
Mahaley's father in a whisper.

Her father nodded and shook the tall
man's hand. After the stranger left,
Mahaley's father sat in front of the
parlor wood stove and smoked his pipe
all evening without saying a word.

Late that night, Mahaley woke up to the sound of the *Belle*'s
steam engine starting. From her window, she looked out at the
Point and saw her father untying the *Belle*. As quietly as she

could, Mahaley left the house and sneaked on board, hiding
behind the animal crates. If her father was going across the river
to Scotchman's Dock, she might have a chance to see Flora.

Mr. Hutchison steered the *Belle* across the river in the dark.
When the boat reached Scotchman's Dock, Mahaley saw a group
of people hiding in the brambles near the stream where she and
Flora liked to swim.

They moved toward the *Belle* very quietly, and as they came aboard, Mahaley saw that all of them, except the tall man in the shiny boots and hat, were black people. Since the Point was the safest place to cross the river, especially at night, Mahaley was sure they were runaway slaves.

Suddenly, Mahaley heard shouting. A dozen men carrying long sticks ran toward the *Belle* from behind Scotchman's store. Mahaley's father quickly started the *Belle*'s steam engine, and the boat pulled away from the dock. The bow bumped against the wooden pier, and Mahaley, who was hiding at the end of the boat near the edge, fell off the boat and into the river.

Because of the shouting, no one heard Mahaley fall into the water. She paddled toward the pier and watched the *Belle of the Point* cross to the Ohio side of the river. The group of runaway slaves were safe, and Mahaley was glad her father had helped them.

When she reached the shore, she climbed out to the pier, shivering and wet. Her canvas slippers had come off in the water, and her feet were caked with river mud.

When Flora's father came outside to see what the trouble was, the men who had tried to stop the slaves scattered in all directions. As Mr. Scotchman turned to go back inside, he looked toward the pier and saw Mahaley.

"My God," he whispered in the dark, but he said it loudly enough for Mahaley to hear. "You might have been hurt, young lady," he scolded. He took her by the hand and led her toward the house.

Flora was awake and had watched from the window. She squealed with happiness when Mahaley came in. Flora hugged her, even though Mahaley was soaking wet.

"I thought I'd never see you again," Flora told her friend.

"I wouldn't be here if I hadn't fallen!" Mahaley explained, and she told them how the *Belle* had bumped the pier and knocked her into the water. Mrs. Scotchman made the girls sassafras tea, and they sat by the fireplace, whispering and giggling and holding hands.

"You'll be missed soon, and your father will be back to fetch you," Mr. Scotchman said to Mahaley. "He was lucky to get away from those men. He's done a dangerous thing."

"Let it pass, Francis, please!" Flora's mother pleaded. But Mr. Scotchman lowered his head and didn't answer. He went outside to light the kerosene lantern that would signal Mahaley's father to return.

Soon, they heard the *Belle of the Point* chugging back across the river to Scotchman's Dock. Mahaley and Flora ran out into the dark to watch the *Belle* tie up at the pier, and Flora's parents followed behind them.

The two girls stood with their arms around each other as Mahaley's father lowered the *Belle*'s loading plank to the shore.

The two men looked at each other but said nothing as Mahaley climbed on board her father's ferryboat. There was a lot of sadness in their eyes, and Mahaley wished there was something that would make them friends again, even though the war had changed everything else.

As the *Belle of the Point* turned back toward the Ohio side of the river, Mahaley and Flora each held her half of the tin heart in her hand. The stern of the *Belle* disappeared from sight of the pier at Scotchman's Dock, but the girls waved to one another in the dark.

They already knew what their fathers were just beginning to understand. Not the river, not even the war, was strong enough to keep the two halves of a tin heart, of a friendship, apart forever.

Atheneum
Macmillan Publishing Company
866 Third Avenue, New York, NY 10022
Collier Macmillan Canada, Inc.
First Edition
Printed in Singapore

10 9 8 7 6 5 4 3 2 1

Library of Congress Cataloging-in-Publication Data
Ackerman, Karen.
The tin heart / by Karen Ackerman;
illustrated by Michael Hays.—1st ed.   p.   cm.
Summary: As the onset of the Civil War causes a rift between their
fathers, Mahaley and Flora find a way to preserve their friendship.
ISBN 0-689-31461-2
[1. Friendship—Fiction.   2. United States—History—Civil War,
1861–1865–Fiction.]   I. Hays, Michael, ill.   II. Title.
PZ7.A1824Ti 1990 [E]—dc19
89-6528 CIP AC